The Elevator Family Goes Abroad

You might enjoy these other titles by Douglas Evans:

The Elevator Family   *Delacorte Press*

The Elevator Family Takes a Hike   *WT Melon*

The Classroom at the End of the Hall   *Front Street*

Math Rash and Other Classroom Tales   *Front Street*

Mouth Moths, More Classroom Tales   *Front Street*

Apple Island, or the Truth About Teachers *Front Street*

MVP: Magellan Voyage Project   *Front Street*

WT Melon
www.wtmelon.com

"good stories; good tunes"

The Elevator Family Goes Abroad

WT Melon
www.wtmelon.com

"good phones, good tunes"

WT Melon Website

Elevator Family Song

For the Bayleys

Christmastime in London and a large crowd had gathered outside Harrods Department Store. People streaming from the Knightsbridge Tube Station joined the crowd. More people stared out the windows of a red double-decker bus passing on Brompton Street. What were they looking at? What was the attraction? The twinkling Christmas lights and evergreen garland bordering the display windows? The Salvation Army band playing carols by a large copper kettle?

"What's all the fuss about?" asked a man, holding a black umbrella against the light rain.

"Dunno," answered a woman in a tan trench coat. "Could be a visit from one of the royals."

A London bobby wearing a sharp blue uniform and a tall round hat pushed through the crowd

"Make way there," he said, holding up his wooden stick. "Step aside please."

When the policeman reached the large window, he looked through the glass and frowned. Inside the display was the same furniture as yesterday—a sofa, a leather chair, a queen-sized bed, and a bed stand—all on sale at a good price. The same evergreen wreath hung above the fake fireplace, and the same Christmas tree stood in the corner.

This morning, however, four people—a man, a woman, a boy, and a girl were asleep in the bed. An unfamiliar sign, a knitted sampler that read: HOME SWEAT HOME, also hung next to the wreath.

The bobby tapped on the window with his stick.

"Hallo? Hallo?" he said, loud enough to be heard through the glass. "What's this all about then?"

The man in the bed sat up. He wore an old-fashioned gray nightshirt and nightcap. He yawned and scratched his large belly.

When the man noticed the crowd on the sidewalk, he waved. "Greetings, Londoners," he called out. "How kind of you to show up this morning to welcome us to England. Only the best."

The people on the sidewalk waved back and smiled.

The bobby frowned. "Coo, so you are Yanks?" he said.

"No, we are the Wilsons from America," said the man in bed. "I'm Walter Wilson." He elbowed the woman next to him. "And is my wonderful wife, Winona. And next to her are my twin son and daughter, Winslow and Whitney."

Now Winona Wilsons sat up and rubbed her eyes with her knuckles. "My, my," she said. "We read that the English people were friendly, but we had no idea. What a wonderful way to start our Christmas Eve here in London."

The people outside cheered. This woke up the girl

and boy in bed.

"Fantabulous," said Winslow Wilson, waving to the crowd.

"Season's greetings," said Whitney Wilson. She grabbed a large book, *Let's Go London*, off the nightstand and began to read. "*London, England, the capital of the United Kingdom. Located on the Thames River. Population of 8,174,100.*"

Again the crowd cheered.

"Up and at'em, family," said Walter. "Time to get dressed."

"Time for some sightseeing," said Winona. "And there are plenty of sights to see."

"Coo! Hold on there, Wilsons," said the policeman. "You're not going anywhere until I sort this out. Just how long have you been in there?"

"We arrived in London last night after an excellent airplane flight," said Walter. "We were packed in the coach section of the plane with hundreds of wonderful people. Tight and cozy, just the way we Wilsons like it."

"And from the Heathrow Airport we rode on the underground train, the *Tube*, as you call it," said Winona. "How exciting. Compact and speedy."

"We searched all over town for a place to stay," said Winslow. "But being the night before Christmas Eve all the hotels were full. We were lucky to find this small room vacant."

"What other room has such a large front window?" said Whitney. "Such modern furniture, and it was even decorated for Christmas."

The police officer pushed back his tall helmet with a thumb. "Coo," he said. "I know what this is. A publicity stunt, isn't it. Harrods put you in there to attract people to the store, didn't they?" He pointed to the crowd with his bobby stick. "And it seems to have done the job."

"Guests are always welcome where the Wilsons stay," said Walter.

"Right-o!" said the bobby. "Well, I need to contact the store manager, so we can somehow manage this crowd. Cheerio for now!"

"And Corn Flakes to you, fine fellow!" said Walter.

By this time several other bobbies had arrived to help control the crowd. The people cheered again as the four Wilsons rose from the bed and left the little room behind the glass. They returned shortly wearing identical khaki pants and blue wool sweaters. While the twins straightened the blankets on the bed, Winona packed the family's wheeled luggage bags, and Walter removed the HOME SWEAT HOME sampler from the mantel.

"Home Sweat Home hangs wherever the Wilsons stay," he said. "And this was one of the finest places

13

ever."

As he spoke, a short, slender man in a well-fitted black suit stepped into the room. A thin mustache wiggled beneath his large red nose. The bobby from outside accompanied him.

"Good morning, sir," the man said to Walter. "I am Sir Cyril Circle, the store manager.

"Morning, back to you, Sir Cyril," said Walter. He held out a hand that the man didn't shake. "Excellent accommodations you have here. Only the best."

"We were very lucky that it was available," said Winona.

"Comfy bed," said Whitney.

"And a fantabulous view," said Winslow.

"Right," the manager said. "But staying here any longer is unacceptable."

"No doubt a special room like this is already booked for Christmas Eve," said Winona. "We were just leaving."

"We want to explore all of London," said Whitney, holding up her travel guide.

Sir Cyril Circle inspected the room and saw that nothing was missing. He peered out the window and saw the enormous crowd. To the bobby, he said, "Everything seems in order, and these Americans have attracted a considerable crowd to the store. Perhaps I will drop the charges."

Walter reached for his wallet. "No charges? Humbug!" he said. "The Wilsons always pay for the rooms they stay in."

Sir Cyril Circle shook his head. "There will be no charges," he said firmly. To the bobby he added, "Yanks. You never know what to expect from them."

"Now then, gentlemen," said Walter. "We're all packed, so we will leave this fine place."

"Merry Christmas to you both," said Winona.

The four Wilsons grabbed the handles of their wheeled travel bags. They left the little room, pulling their luggage behind them.

Shortly afterward, they exited the store through a revolving door. When the crowd spotted them, they cheered louder than ever.

"Thank you. Thank you," Walter said.

"Happy Christmas to you," the Londoners called back.

Winona dropped a pound coin into the copper kettle beside the Salvation Army band. "And thank you for providing such wonderful wake-up music this morning," she said.

In single file, the Wilsons walked down the sidewalk. The day was cloudy, a bit chilly, but the rain had stopped.

"So many sights to see," said Whitney, consulting her guidebook. "Big Ben, the Tower of London, the British Museum."

"And don't forget we must find a place to stay tonight," said Winona.

Winslow pointed to a small red hut standing on the street corner. Small windows filled all four sides. Inside a woman was talking on a telephone.

"Fantabulous," said Winslow. "Wouldn't that be a great place to stay?"

"Too bad it's already taken," said Walter. "Let's

move on. Perhaps we'll find another one just like it."

At the street corner, the Wilsons stood before a zebra-striped crosswalk. The instant Walter stepped into the street, a horn honked as a red double-decker bus zoomed past.

"Great Scott!" he exclaimed. "That bus is driving on the wrong side of the street."

"Don't forget, Dad," said Whitney. "In Great Britain, they drive on the left side of the road."

Walter tugged on the bottom of his sweater. "Well, in America we drive on the *right* side," he said indignantly. "Why would the English want to do anything differently?"

A short walk through a park brought the Wilsons to tall iron gates outside a large wide building. Two Christmas wreaths hung on the closed gates.

"Buckingham Palace," Whitney announced. "This is where Queen Elizabeth lives." She pointed to the Union Jack flying above the palace roof. "The British flag flying over the palace means the queen is at home."

"But her home is so big!" said Winona. "Why

would the queen need all those rooms?"

"775 rooms to be exact," said Whitney, reading from her guidebook.

"Maybe she enjoys having a lot of guests," said Walter.

To his left, Winslow spotted a tall narrow building with the golden letters ER stenciled in the peak of its slanted roof

"Now that's a more practical place to live," he said.

A man stood erect before the building's front doorway. He wore a bright red uniform, and a tall furry hat sat on his head. A rifle rested on his shoulder.

The four Wilsons walked up to the man.

"Greetings, sir," said Walter. "We were just admiring your little house."

"We are looking for a similar room to stay in tonight," said Winona.

The man stared forward. He remained silent and standing yardstick straight.

"We understand," said Walter. "It must be

humbling living so close to the queen and having a finer home."

Still, the man in red said nothing.

A car horn honked behind the Wilsons. They turned to see a black taxicab parked nearby. The driver, a man of about thirty, had a thin black beard and wore a blue turban. He leaned out the window and said, "You won't get a word out of that fellow, my friends? May I help you?"

"We are the Wilsons," said Walter.

"We're looking for a place to stay tonight," said Winona.

The driver nodded. "Rooms are hard to find in the city this time of year, my friends," he said. "But I know a small bed and breakfast south of the river that might have something available."

"Excellent," said Walter. "We want only the best."

The four Wilsons climbed into the back seat of the taxicab.

"Isn't this exciting," said Whitney. "Our first ride in a London cab."

"This taxi is about the size of the room, Toll 4, that we stayed in on the bridge over the Mississippi River," said Winslow.

"I'm Walter Wilson," Walter said to the driver. "My wife Winona and our twins Whitney and Winslow complete the family. We are from America."

"You don't say," said the driver. "My name is Samir. I come from a region in India called Punjab. I take you now to a fine B&B."

He turned on the taximeter and slowly pulled away from the Buckingham Palace gate.

"Now sit back, my friends," he said. "And enjoy the view of London."

The black taxicab took the Wilsons down a broad straight road lined with tall trees, each decorated with twinkling Christmas trees.

"This is called *The Mall*," Samir told them.

The family pressed their faces against the windows of the cab, admiring the Christmasy view.

Walter noticed a laptop computer on the seat beside the driver. "I'm guessing that you do other things besides drive a taxi, Samir," he said.

Samir looked in the rearview mirror. "You are correct, my friend," he said. "I'm trying to write a novel. I wish to be a writer."

"Fantabulous," said Winslow.

"You must get a lot of ideas and meet many interesting people, driving around London," said Whitney.

Samir nodded. "You are correct, and I put all my ideas into my laptop. Trouble is, my friend, so far I can't put all those ideas together to make a good story."

"I understand, Samir," said Walter. "You have what writers call Writer's Block."

"Having a clogged brain must be frustrating," said Winona.

"That is correct, my friends," Samir said. "But I must not concern you with my problems. You are here to enjoy London at Christmastime."

At this point, the taxi drove through a tall arch and entered a large square. In the center of the square stood a tall Christmas tree next to a taller pillar with a bronze statue on top. Milling around the tree and pillar were a few dozen people feeding an equal number of pigeons.

"Trafalgar Square," Samir announced.

"And on top of that column is a statue of Admiral Nelson, a famous British sea admiral," said Whitney, checking her guidebook.

"Coo! Coo!" the Wilsons called to the pigeons out the taxi windows.

Coo! Coo! Coo! the pigeons called back.

Next Samir drove down another straight road that he called Whitehall.

"And there's 10 Downy Street where the Prime Minister lives," noted Whitney, pointing out the window.

"And up ahead is Big Ben," said Samir.

As the cab drove past the famous clock tower, the Wilsons heard the famous chime.

Bong! Bong! Bong! Bong!

Bong! Bong! Bong! Bong!

"Ten o'clock," Walter said, reading off the big clock face.

"Westminster Bridge," Samir announced, as he drove onto a bridge that crossed the Thames River.

The Wilsons, however, weren't looking at the river or the colorful lights strung along the bridge. They were staring at a giant Ferris wheel that stood on the south bank. In place of seats, small glass rooms were attached to the enormous wheel. Slowly the wheel revolved, taking the rooms high into the air.

"Fantabulous!" said Winslow.

"It's perfect!" said Winona.

"Only the best!" said Walter.

"Oh, I hope a room is available for tonight," said Whitney.

"That is the London Eye," Samir said, into the rearview mirror. "Do you want me to let you off here so you can take a ride?"

"Yes!" the Wilsons chorused.

Samir pulled the black cab over to the curb. Walter handed him the fare with a big tip. "Good luck with your novel, Samir," he said.

"May you get unblocked soon," said Winona.

"Thank you," said the driver. "I now have more good characters and ideas to put into my laptop."

After the taxi drove away, the four Wilsons ran up to the London Eye. They couldn't keep their eyes off the small glass rooms that were slowly rising into the air.

"We might be in luck," said Winona. "Some of the rooms are empty."

"The view from on top might beat the view we had in the little cabin on top of Mt. Baldy," said Winslow.

"Remember the fire we spotted from up there?" said Whitney.

"A room for four," Walter said to the woman in

the ticket booth. "Only the best for the Wilsons."

"There you go, Love," said the woman, handing Walter the tickets.

The Wilsons entered one of the oval-shaped rooms that stopped in front of them. The glass door closed, and the room slowly began to rise.

"Fantabulous," said Winslow. "Just like the Otis Room we stayed in at the San Francisco Hotel. It has its ups and downs."

"We can see all of London from here," said Whitney. "There's Big Ben. There's Trafalgar Square. There's Buckingham Palace."

"I say we hang our Home Sweat Home sign right here and now," said Walter.

"But it's only ten in the morning," said Winona. "I know the London Eye would be a wonderful place to stay, but we have so much of the city still to see."

The Wilsons grew silent, admiring the view.

Finally, when the little room paused at the top of the wheel, Walter said, "Winona is right. Why be hasty about picking a place to stay. We can always come back here if we want."

The little room began to descend. When the glass room reached the ground again, the family exited.

"London is so full of wonderful places to stay it's hard to choose," Winona said to the ticket woman on the way out.

"Cheerio, Love," said the woman.

"And Corn Flakes to you," said Walter.

The Wilsons walked along the riverbank. Christmas lights connected the iron light posts they passed. Under a bridge, they paused to listen to a teenaged girl who was playing a guitar and singing *Christmas Is Coming*. Her freckled face was thin and pale. She wore a long red dress and her red hair hung down from the brim of her red felt hat. By her feet lay an opened guitar case, but few people were dropping in coins. Few even stopped to listen to the caroler.

"Poor dear," Winona whispered to Walter and the twins. "She's not making much money."

"No wonder," Walter returned. "Her singing is excellent, but her guitar playing..." He made a face.

"...is dreadful."

"It's out of tune and off the beat," said Winslow.

"She's not even holding the guitar correctly," said Whitney.

When the girl stopped playing, the Wilsons walked up to her. Walter dropped a pound coin into her guitar case.

The girl smiled. "Ta," she said. "Enough for a cup of tea." She spoke with a Scottish accent.

"You have a beautiful voice, young lady," said Winona.

"Only the best," said Walter.

"Ta," the girl repeated. "I wish other people thought so. I've been busking in London for over a week, and I've only made a few quid."

The Wilsons exchanged looks.

Walter pointed to the girl's guitar. "Um, have you been playing that instrument for long?" he asked.

"Since this morning," she answered. "Yesterday I tried playing the accordion while singing, but I made even less money. I moved to London to study singing at the Royal College of Music, but I won't be able to stay if I can't pay tuition. Happy Christmas to you."

"Merry Christmas to you," the Wilsons said as one.

The girl started singing *Deck the Halls* while strumming her guitar more off the beat than before.

"Poor, dear," said Winona, as the Wilsons resumed their walk along the river. "I wish I knew a way to help her."

"I wish I had earplugs," said Walter, wincing. "Fa la la la oh oh oh."

Soon the Wilsons came to a small cafe with outdoor tables.

"Time for a spot of tea," said Walter.

The family sat at a table and looked around. Nearby stood another busker, a man of about eighteen, playing

the guitar. He wore a green hoodie and a green wool cap. A patch of brown hair, the color of weak tea, lay under his lower lip. Like the other singer, an opened guitar case lay by his feet, and like the other singer, this case held few coins. Unlike the girl, however, this man's guitar playing was excellent. He played a lovely intro to *Silent Night*, before starting to sing.

"Oh, dear," said Winona.

"Oh, my," said Whitney.

"Oh, no," said Winslow.

"Oh, oh, oh," said Walter. "He sings like a donkey with a cold."

Walter flicked a pound coin into the guitar case, and the busker stopped singing.

"Thanks," he said. "That's more money than I've made in the past three hours."

"It was worth it," said Walter. "We're the Wilsons from America.

"Please to meet you, Wilsons," said the man. "I'm Kevin."

"Your playing is first-rate, Kevin," said Winona.

"Thanks," said Kevin. "I've been playing since before I could walk. I moved to London to study guitar at the Royal College of Music. But if I don't make more money busking I will need to move back to Wales. I just don't know what the problem is."

The Wilsons exchanged looks. They all had the same idea. Why couldn't the girl and Kevin play together? With her singing and his guitar playing, they would make a winning combo.

Walter spoke first. "Kevin, we were just about to have a cup of tea and a sandwich. Would you like to join us?"

"You look like you could use a bite to eat," said Winona.

Kevin licked his lips. "Sure could," he said. "Haven't eaten in a while."

The teenager placed his guitar in the case and sat down with the Wilsons. While Walter went inside to order, Winslow took off to fetch the other singer.

Soon Walter returned with cups of tea, cucumber sandwiches, and packets of potato chips.

"Great Scott," he said. "The server called these potato chips *crisps* and he called some French fries *chips*. Why do English people make our language so difficult?"

When Winslow returned with the girl singer, she frowned at Kevin.

"Hello, Verity," Kevin said. "I didn't know you were also invited to lunch."

"Excellent," said Walter. "So you two know each other."

The girl sat at the table. "We attend the same music school," she said.

"Verity sings every day under the Hungerford Bridge," said Kevin. "People must give her all their change before they get to me."

"That's not how I see it," said Verity. "Each day Kevin sings near this café, and the people must give *him* all their coins before they have a chance to hear *me*."

Together, the four Wilsons took a sip of tea.

"That's not how we see it," said Walter.

Walter handed Kevin and Verity a cucumber sandwich. They champed into them as if this were their first meal in days.

Winona sipped some tea and nodded to her husband.

"Curious, you two young people are competing for the same audience," Walter said.

"And you have the same goals," said Winona.

Kevin swallowed hard. "But thanks to Verity, I'm not making much money."

Verity shook her head. "It's Kevin's fault that I

only make a few pounds each morning."

"Then why don't you combine your talents?" said Walter

"Become partners!" asked Winona.

"A duet!" Winslow and Whitney said together.

Kevin sneered. "Um, what do you mean exactly?"

"You mean play together?" asked Verity.

"Verity, your singing is outstanding," said Walter. "But quite frankly, your guitar playing… isn't so great. On the other hand, Kevin, you're an expert guitar player, but your singing makes my toes curl."

"It's a perfect match," said Winona.

"Verity can sing," said Whitney.

"While you, Kevin, can accompany her on the guitar," said Winslow.

The two buskers stared at each other. They bit into their sandwiches again and studied each other some more.

Finally, Kevin said, "Blimey! That might work."

"Yes, it might," said Verity. "I say we give it a go."

"Cheers!" said Wilson, raising their teacups.

The two young people stood. Kevin grabbed his guitar from the case and Verity stood beside him.

"How about *Holly and the Ivy*?" she said.

Kevin nodded and began to play. Verity joined in with her beautiful vocals.

The result was astonishing. Every person walking along the riverbank stopped to listen. Soon pound coins went flying into the guitar case. When the pair finished the carol, the listeners burst into applause. Verity bowed, and Kevin began playing *Busking by the Thames*.

Meanwhile, the Wilsons stood up from the table.

"A perfect combination," said Winslow.

"Green and red," said Whitney. "They even look good together."

Walter bit into a potato chip. "Crisps! Humbug!" he said. "I still don't see why the English need to change the name of things."

Busking by the Thames

Verity:
He played like a rock star, but his guitar case was empty.
His strumming was fine, but he sang three keys out of key.
Then I started to sing, and his solo song became two.
Now I'm busking by the banks of the Thames with my friend you.
Kevin:
She sang like a bird, but no one stopped to hear her song.
Her voice so sweet, but she strummed the guitar all wrong.
Then I started to play and her solo song became two.
Now I'm busking by the banks of the Thames with my friend you.
Both:
We still sing and play each day but never alone.
Our hat's been full since the London crowds have grown.
We're the duo you'll find beneath the bridge to Waterloo.
Busking by the banks of the Thames with my friend you.

(Listen to Busking by the Thames)

Whitney consulted her guidebook. "Tower of London next," she said.

"There's an underground station across the river," said Winslow.

The family grabbed the handles of their wheeled luggage. They waved farewell to Verity and Kevin and climbed the stairs up to the Waterloo Bridge. From below they heard the buskers singing *Silver Bells.*

"Bravo," said Walter.

"They've drawn quite a crowd," said Winona.

"Perfect harmony," said Winslow.

"They should have enough tuition money in no time," said Whitney.

In single file, the Wilsons started across the bridge. Halfway across, it started to rain. Fortunately, a man on the bridge was selling umbrellas out of a white bucket.

"Four please," Walter said to him. "Only the best."

"Four of the best brollies in London for you, mate," said the man.

He handed a black umbrella to each of the Wilsons who popped them open. As they continued across the bridge, they were surprised to hear their names called out in an American accent.

"Hello, Wilsons! Walter! Winona! Whitney and Winslow! Hello, Elevator Family!"

At first, the Wilsons didn't recognize the man standing before them. He wore a long brown coat over a brown suit and was holding a large brown umbrella. Joining him under the umbrella were a

blond-haired woman and a girl of about ten. They also

wore brown coats.

"It's me," the man said. "Bob Brown from the San Francisco Hotel. We had dinner together in your Otis room."

All four Wilsons realized who this man was at the same time. "Mr. Brown!" they said together.

Yes, the very businessman who the Wilsons had met in San Francisco was now standing before them in London, England. In fact, Mr. Brown was the person who coined the nickname the Elevator Family.

"Good to see you again, Robert," said Walter.

Mr. Brown put his arm around the woman and girl. "Wilsons, please meet my wife, Bonnie and my daughter Becky. Bonnie and Becky, meet the Wilson family—Walter, Winona, Whitney, and Winslow."

The girl's eyes went wide. "Oh my gosh! The Wilsons?" she said. "You're the Elevator Family? Oh my gosh! You're the family who rescued the kidnapped girl in the San Francisco Hotel where my Dad stayed. Oh my gosh! You're famous. I have a doll of each of you and a lunchbox with your picture on it."

"You're the family, who made it possible for our family to spend more time together," said Bonnie Brown.

"So your fad selling business must be going well, Mr. Brown," said Winona.

"As Winslow always says, it's been *fantabulous*," Bob Brown said. "Ever since you allowed me to use your name, *The Elevator Family*, on toys and other merchandise, I've been working for myself. That's what I'm doing on this side of the pond. The Brits are interested in licensing *The Elevator Family* brand. Soon your picture will be in magazines, video games, and T-shirts all over Great Britain."

"Let's all go to a pub and catch up on things," said Bonnie Brown.

"Oh my gosh! That would be so cool," said Becky Brown.

"Love to, but we have a busy day," said Walter.

"We're looking for another ideal place to stay tonight on Christmas Eve," said Winona.

"Right now we're taking the Tube to see the Tower

of London," said Whitney.

"Isn't the underground fantabulously tight and compact?" said Winslow.

Mr. Brown burst out laughing. "The London Underground and the Elevator Family! That's brilliant." The man held out a business card. "Anyway, here's my address in London and cell phone number. Please keep in touch."

"Pleased to meet you," said Bonnie Brown.

"Oh my gosh! I can't believe I met the Elevator Family," said Becky Brown. "Oh my gosh! You look just like my four dolls."

The Wilsons stood at the entrance of the Embankment Tube Station. A stream of people holding umbrellas rushed past.

"I've been looking forward to getting back on the underground train all morning," said Winona.

"Hundreds of other people are rushing to get on as well," said Walter.

Whitney checked the London Underground map on the wall. "We must take the Circle Line to reach the Tower of London," she said.

Full of excitement, the Wilsons bought their tickets

and took an escalator down to the subway platform. The subway train arrived shortly. Doors in front of the Wilsons slid open, and they surged into a crowded car with a dozen other people. All the seats were full, so the family stood by the door.

"So tight and cozy," said Winona.

"This is as fun as when we stayed in the long narrow cabin next to a baseball diamond," said Winslow.

"Or when we stayed in the small room in the back of our fifth-grade classroom," said Whitney.

"Greetings, everyone," Walters called to the people standing beside him. "We're the Wilsons from America."

The car jolted, and Walter quickly grabbed a strap hanging overhead.

"We're off completely!" he said.

As the subway car sped down a dark round tunnel, the four Wilsons studied their neighbors. A man in a pin-striped suit stood on one side of them reading the London Times. A woman dressed in a colorful sari stood on the other.

Several young people wore backpacks, but one man, in particular, caught their attention. He sat in the aisle on an orange pack. He wore new hiking shoes, new blue jeans, and a new leather jacket. The scruffy growth of hair his chin appeared new as well.

"Greetings, young man," Walter said. "Looks, like you've been doing a bit of traveling."

The teenagers glanced toward Walter but said nothing.

"Where are you from?" Winona asked.

A look of fear crossed the boy's face. "New York," he answered weakly.

"Next stop, Temple Tube Station," announced Whitney, who had memorized the entire Circle Line.

The subway stopped. The doors opened and people piled out after which more people piled in. The train started up again and Walter again addressed the teenager.

"How long have you been traveling, my boy?"

The boy hesitated before answering. "I'm traveling

around the world for a year." Then he lowered his head. "But I just started my trip."

"Blackfriars Tube Station," Whitney called out. "Aren't these names fun?"

Again the train stopped to let people out and in.

"Just started traveling? So have we," Walter said to the teenager. "After Christmas, we'll visit the continent."

"Now we're looking for just the right small cozy place to stay in for Christmas Eve," said Winona. "So many to choose from."

Suddenly the boy's face lit up. "I know you," he said. "You're the Elevator Family. I've read comic books about your adventures."

"That's us, my boy," said Walter.

"Gosh, imagine I'm standing with the Elevator Family right here in London," said the boy. "My name's Alex, and to tell you the truth, so far my trip hasn't gone well." When he said this his face scrunched up, and his eyes watered.

Winona put a hand on his shoulder. "What's

troubling you, Alex?" she said. "Maybe we can help."

"Cannon Street Tube Station," Whitney announced, as the train slowed down again.

"You see, I'm taking a year off after high school to travel around the world alone," Alex said. "But I've never been to another country before."

"Brave of you, my boy," said Walter.

"Go on, Alex," said Winona. "Tell us what happened."

"Well, you see, this morning I took the underground from the airport. But when I got off and went up to the street, I panicked. I was scared. Everything seemed so different—the stores, the signs, the accents, and the traffic."

"Yes, the British do seem to enjoy doing things differently," said Walter. "Do you know they call potato chips *crisps*?"

"Go on, Alex," said Winona giving Walter a look.

The boy stood. "So, you see, instead of finding the Bloomsbury Youth Hostel where I was planning to stay, I came right back down to the subway station. I've been riding in this subway car for the past four hours, trying to get up the nerve to return to the streets."

"Poor, dear," said Winona.

"Around and around on the Circle Line," said Winslow.

"Monument Tube Station," said Whitney.

Alex nodded. "Yes, I've passed this tube station seven times already," he said.

"Just a bit of travel jitters, that's all, my boy," said Walter. "Nothing serious."

"That's right," said Winona. "Traveling alone takes courage, and I'm sure it has its rewards."

"The day after Christmas I'm supposed to leave for Paris," Alex said. "After that, I was planning on traveling through Europe and then Africa and then Asia and then Australia."

"And you just need a little push to get started," said Whitney.

"So maybe we can help," said Winslow. "Alex, do you want us to go with you to the youth hostel? We can help you check in."

"Excellent idea," said Walter. "Once you're with fellow travelers, the old traveling nerve will come back."

Alex smiled for the first time. "Oh, would you mind?"

"It's better than going around and around the Circle Line all Christmas Eve," said Winona.

"Tower of London Tube Station," Whitney announced, as the train slowed down once more.

"But that's not for us," said Winslow. "We're circling all the way around to Bloomsbury."

"Wow, thanks, Elevator Family," Alex said. "Wait until I tell my family who I met on my first day in London."

"Let's hope this is just the first of your many adventures," said Winona.

"Only the best," said Walter.

●●●

Circle Line
(based on the tune Lilliberleo)

Around and around London I go,
Seeing the city from down below.
First trip abroad, gives me a scare.
I'm too nervous to go up there.

Chorus:
But it's safe and sound on the Underground.
I ride the Tube around and around.
At each stop I read the sign.
Everything's fine on the Circle Line.

Under Victoria; Under Tower Hill
Under Westminster was a thrill.
I went up top in Camden Town.
Took one look and came straight back down.
Chorus:

I'll be in London for one more day.
I must see the sights; I must see a play.
But where can I sleep? What do I eat?
How to pay in pounds or cross a street?
Chorus:

(Listen to Circle Line)

After escorting Alex to the Bloomsbury Youth Hostel, the Wilsons found themselves walking through a pleasant park called Russell Square. The rain had stopped, so the family lowered their umbrellas.

"Fantabulous," said Winslow, pointing to a corner of the square. "There's one of those small red houses with a telephone in it, and that one is empty."

"We still have plenty of time to find accommodations," said Winona.

"We still have plenty of sights to see," said

Whitney, checking *Let's Go London.*

In the center of the square stood a tall Christmas tree wrapped with blue twinkling lights. Next to the tree stood a man selling roasted chestnuts from a cart. Walter ordered four bags, and the family sat on a bench to eat their snacks.

On the bench next to them sat a young woman dressed in a black and white nanny's uniform. A large baby pram stood before her. As the Wilsons ate their nuts, a baby in the pram started to cry. At the same time, the nanny cried as well. The baby cried louder drowning out the nanny, and then the nanny cried louder, drowning out the baby. The baby wailed louder still and the woman did likewise.

"Merry Christmas, madam," Walter called out.

The nanny looked toward the Wilsons. She dabbed her eyes with a handkerchief. "Happy Christmas to you," she said.

" *Whaah,*" went the baby and again the nanny began crying.

"What seems to be the problem?" asked Winona

The woman sniffed. "I can't seem to keep Victoria quiet."

"We're the Wilsons from America," said Walter. He held out his bag of chestnuts. "Care for a nut."

The nanny shook her head. "My name is Mary, and yesterday I started working for Lord and Lady Harold Hashtag. If Lord and Lady Hashtag find out that I can't stop Victoria from crying, they will surely replace me."

Again Mary sniffed and buried her face in her hands.

"*Whaah!*" went Victoria.

"See what I mean," said the nanny, and she cried some more.

"That kid has a great pair of lungs," said Walter.

The Wilsons sat silently eating their chestnuts, listening to the nanny and baby cry. Mary cried and then Victoria cried. The woman cried some more and the baby did the same.

"Madam, I think I have the answer to your problem," Walter said at length.

The nanny looked up with red eyes. "What do you mean?"

"I think little Victoria might be a copycat baby," Walter said.

Mary looked worried. "Oh, dear, is that an illness?" she asked.

Then she started to sob some more, and at the same time Victoria let out her loudest wail yet.

"*Whaaaaaaah!*"

"No, Mary," said Winona. "Walter just means Victoria is copying what you do. The reason she cries is that you cry. She's copying your behavior.

The nanny's face went blank. "You don't mean that's all I was doing wrong?"

The Wilsons nodded.

The nanny smiled. The baby grinned in the same manner. Then Mary laughed, and so did Victoria.

"She's laughing. Victoria Hashtag is laughing," Mary said. She clapped her hands, and the baby also clapped. "All day long I thought I was a terrible nanny, but this whole time the baby was only copying me."

"She must like you," said Whitney. "She's watching everything you do."

"Copying is a form of flattery," said Winslow.

The nanny stood. It had begun to drizzle again, so she opened a large black umbrella. "I don't know how to thank you, Wilson family," she said. "From now on I'll be extra careful how I act around Victoria."

"Happy to be of service," said Walter

"Lord and Lady Hashtag are very lucky," said Winona.

The nanny held her umbrella above her head. The Wilsons were half-expecting her to fly away, Mary-Poppins style. Instead, she said, "Happy Christmas to you," and strode briskly down the walk, pushing the baby pram before her.

"Excellent," said Walter. "Time to head to the Tower of London."

"The Russell Square Tube Station is close by," said Whitney.

The Wilsons rose from the bench and raised their umbrellas. Near the park exit, they spotted a slender man dressed as Santa Claus standing on a wooden box. His outfit included a baggy red shirt and pants, a floppy red hat, and a bushy gray beard that appeared real. A tin cup filled with pound coins lay next to the box he stood upon.

"Remember, Christmas is a time of giving, ladies and gents," the man said to the small crowd that had gathered to hear him. "So please give all you can to Father Christmas. Father Christmas appreciates any coin you can spare. Happiness doesn't result from what we get, but from what we give. So make yourself happy, and give to Father Christmas."

Walter pulled on his chin. "That man has a knack for salesmanship," he said to his family. He took a pound coin from his pocket and flicked it into the tin cup.

"Thank you, Governor," the man said. "Happy Christmas."

"Now here's a switch," Walter replied. "Santa Claus asking for presents instead of presenting them."

The man stepped down from his box. "Times are

difficult in this country, Governor," he said. "Jobs are hard to come by. Thankfully there are plenty of good people like you in the city who will give a needy fellow like me a few bob." He held out a hand that Walter shook. "Me name is Jack, Jack Christmas. People call me Father Christmas?"

"We're the Wilsons from America," said Winona.

"Father Christmas, we were admiring your knack for drawing a crowd," said Walter.

"Thank you, Governor," said the man. "I enjoy people."

Walter turned toward his family and said something no one else heard.

"Walter, that's wonderful," said Winona.

"Fantabulous idea," said Winslow.

"Do it, Dad," said Whitney.

"Father Christmas, we know of a job that might be just right for you," Walter said.

A grin spread through the man's grey whiskers. "A job? You have work for me, Governor?"

Walter pulled Mr. Brown's business card from his

pocket.

"Our friend Bob Brown is starting a business here in London," said Winona. "We're sure he needs help."

"Father Christmas, in the states we are known as the Elevator Family," said Winslow.

"We just learned that we're rather popular back home," said Whitney.

"And now Mr. Brown is in England to make us popular here," said Winona.

"And if you can only direct me to the nearest telephone, Jack, I can give him a call," said Walter.

"There's a phone booth on the corner, Governor," the man said. "Any work would be appreciated. Any job would be better than standing on a soapbox all day, wagging my gob."

While Walter made his call to Mr. Brown, the other Wilsons continued to talk with Jack Christmas.

They learned he was a former coal miner in Northern England. After the coal mines closed, he had a hard time finding steady employment. He has been living under London Bridge for over a year.

"It's getting more crowded under that bridge month by month," he said. "Times are hard."

"All set," said Walter, when he returned. "Mr. Brown said to wait right here, Jack. I told him he couldn't miss you. He said he'll get you a place to stay, and you can start work the day after *Boxing Day* whatever that is."

"Boxing Day is the day after Christmas," said Whitney. "Boxing Day is a holiday in England."

Walter shook his umbrella. "Then why can't the British just call it *the day after Christmas* as we do?"

Jack Christmas was so happy with the news of a job he started doing a little dance right there on the pavement.

"I don't know how to thank you, Governor," he said. "You've given Father Christmas the best Christmas present ever."

After a long and enjoyable subway ride, the Wilsons reached Tower Hill Tube Station. Once at the Tower of London's front gate, however, they didn't admire the tower's high stone walls, its tall round towers, or the colorful banners waving from the ramparts. Their attention was fixed on the small brown hut in which a man stood collecting tickets. He wore a red velvet coat with gold stitching, red knee breeches with white stockings, and a black top hat.

"Welcome to the Tower of London and the Crown Jewels," the man said.

"Excellent accommodations you have there, sir," Walter said, nodding toward the hut. "Would you know if another one if available for us to stay in tonight? Only the best. Only the best will do for the Wilson family."

The man gave Walter a quizzical look. "I'm afraid, sir, that these *booths* are for the Beefeaters only."

"How unfortunate," said Winona. "We're vegetarians."

Whitney held up her guidebook. "The Beefeaters are the Tower of London guards," she said. "This man is a Beefeater. He's wearing the traditional Beefeater's uniform."

"That is correct, ma'am," said the man in the hut. "Now enjoy your visit to the Tower. Cheerio."

"And Corn Flakes to you," Walter said.

With a tour map in hand, the Wilsons explored the vast Tower of London grounds. They visited the Traitors Gate, the White Tower, and a grassy area where a Beefeater was feeding the famous tower ravens. In other buildings, the family viewed displays of ancient weapons, shiny amour, and Elizabethan costumes. Most enjoyable of all, however, were the many small rooms they passed.

"This Tower of London doesn't seem like a bad place to stay for a few weeks," said Winona.

Last of all, the Wilsons approached the building housing the Crown Jewels, a large collection of crowns, necklaces, and tiaras covered with precious gems. As they were about to enter the building, two Beefeaters— one tall and the other skinny with big ears—came out. When Walter saw the men's faces, he stopped in his tracks."

"Great Scott," he said. "We've seen those fellows before!"

"Very unlikely, dear," said Winona.

"Hardly, Dad," said Whitney.

"All the Beefeaters look the same," said Winslow.

"No, look quickly before they go away," said Walter. "I know those faces are familiar."

The other Wilsons turned and caught a glimpse of the men. All three jaws dropped.

"Yes, we *have* seen them before," Winona said darkly.

"But they weren't dressed as Beefeaters," said Winslow

"And it wasn't in England," said Whitney.

Walter snapped his finger. "Great Scott!" he said. "They're the bad guys! They're the men who showed up in our San Francisco Otis room, pushing a large trunk."

"They're the kidnappers who kidnapped that kid, Lizzy Chronicle," said Winona.

"But I thought they were in San Quentin Prison," said Winslow.

"No, they're here in the Tower of London dressed as fake Beefeaters," said Whitney. "What could they be up to?"

"No good, no doubt," said Winona. "Could it have something to do to do with the Crown Jewels?"

"Family, we have a mission," said Walter. He held up a finger. "One...we must enter the Crown Jewels gallery." A second finger went up. "Two, we must search for anything suspicious. Anything out of place. Anything missing." He raised a third finger. "And three...we must report our findings to the real Beefeaters. Got it?"

"Got it," said the others.

Once through the doorway, the Wilsons stood in a large dimly-lit room filled with glass display cases. Spotlights in the cases shone upon an abundance of dazzling jewels. Some cases held tall crowns encrusted with diamonds, rubies, emeralds, and sapphires. Others displayed diamond necklaces and emerald earrings.

"A gem of a place," said Walter, to one of the four Beefeaters who stood around the gallery holding long staffs.

The family walked up to the first display case.

"That's the crown Queen Elizabeth II wore on her coronation," said Whitney, reading her guidebook.

They walked to the next case.

"And this is the crown she wears every year at her opening of Parliament," Whitney explained.

"How many crowns does a queen need?" said

Walter.

"Look here," Winslow called out. He stood before a case with nothing in it. "It's empty."

"Could the fake Beefeaters have nipped whatever was in there?" asked Winona.

"This case held the Queen's Christmas brooch," said Whitney. "That's the large pin that Queen Elizabeth wears each Christmas when she delivers her Christmas message on TV." She read more out of her guidebook. "*The Christmas brooch holds one of the largest diamonds in the world. It's called the Star of Bethlehem and it's valued at over one-hundred million pounds or one and a half million US dollars.*"

"So the Christmas brooch and the Star of Bethlehem are missing," said Walter.

"And I bet the two San Francisco robbers have robbed them," said Winona. "We must report this."

The Wilsons hurried up to one of the Beefeater guards.

"Sir, I wish to report a robbery," said Walter.

The Beefeater's eyes opened wide, pushing up his

bushy eyebrows. "What's that then?" he said.

"We believe that the Queen's Christmas brooch has been stolen by two men posing as Beefeaters," said Winona.

"What?" said the guard. "Not likely."

"Then just look over at that display case," said Winslow. "It's empty."

"But don't worry," said Whitney. "We know what the crooks look like."

The Beefeater grinned. "Right, then," he said. "Just some Yankee humor, is this? Well, I'll have you know that the Queen's Christmas brooch hasn't gone missing whatsoever. Currently, it's over at Buckingham Palace, so the Queen can wear it on Christmas tomorrow. I know that for sure. I took it over to the palace myself less than an hour ago."

Walter's face turned Christmas red. "Great Scott," he muttered under his breath.

"Thanks for your concern anyway," said the guard. "And enjoy the rest of your time at the Tower."

The Wilsons returned to the empty display case.

"Still something's fishy," Walter said.

"Why would those two criminals be here in London?" asked Winona.

"Why would they be dressed up as Beefeaters?" said Whitney

"And why were they in this room filled with precious stones?" said Winslow.

"Family, we need another plan," said Walter. He held up one finger and then another. "We must find the fake Beefeaters and follow them."

The others nodded.

"But we must make sure they don't see us," said Winslow. "They know who we are."

"Remember how sour they looked when we had them arrested at the San Francisco Hotel," said Whitney.

The Wilsons left the Crown Jewels room and searched the Tower's large central courtyard. They spotted the two phony Beefeaters entering a building on the far side. This building was off-limits to visitors, so they made sure no real Beefeater was watching as they hurried across the courtyard and entered the building themselves.

Once inside, they stood in a dank, dusty chamber. Apparently, this room had once displayed instruments of torture used in the Tower of London. Iron chains, iron locks, and iron cuffs hung on the walls. Head screws, knee splitters, iron maidens, and various wooden racks stood around the dusty floor.

"Kind of gruesome," Walter whispered.

"Look, footprints," said Winslow, pointing to two sets of shoe tracks on the dusty floor.

Without a sound, the family followed the prints to a wooden door in the back of the room.

Walter held his ear against the door. Hearing voices, he gave the thumbs-up sign, and the others joined him.

The first voice they heard was deep and familiar. It belonged to the tall robber. "I can't wait to get out of this goofy Beefeater's costume," he said. "Why do Tower guards wear these silly outfits anyway?"

"Jeez, quit your beefing," said a second voice, also familiar. This belonged to the skinny thief with big ears. "And careful with that brooch. Remember that one is the real deal."

"It sure was a breeze switching our fake jewelry for this genuine one," said the first crook. "Just look how that big bobble in the middle sparkles."

"And the guards didn't suspect a thing," said the second. "Like I said, the ideal time to make the switch was when the real brooch was out of the case and being transferred to Buckingham Palace. Jeez, my plan worked like a charm."

"On TV tomorrow, the queen will be wearing a pin full of glass stones," said the first man. "I hope the glue doesn't melt under the hot TV lights."

The two men laughed.

"Jeez, the glass pieces would fall out and shatter on the palace floor," said the second thief.

The pair laughed some more.

Meanwhile, outside the door, the Wilsons had heard the whole conversation. Walter nodded and pointed to some chains hanging on the wall. The twins left to retrieve them. Soon the heavy iron links were wrapped around the door handle, locking the two robbers inside the room.

"Well done, family!" said Walter. "Mission accomplished."

"Now we can go fetch the real Beefeaters," said Winona.

"Just wait until they see what new prisoners we have for them in the Tower of London," said Whitney..

In no time, the real Tower of London guards had recovered the real Christmas brooch. The fake Beefeaters had it with them inside a black velvet sack.

The real Beefeaters rushed the real jewelry to Buckingham Palace before Queen Elizabeth put on the fake, tacky brooch. Scotland Yard, the British Police department, was especially glad to have the two American crooks in custody.

Last January the pair had escaped from San Quentin Prison, and, despite being on the FBI's Most Wanted List, they had managed to slip into the United

Kingdom.

But where were the Wilsons? What had happened to the remarkable family who had captured the thieves? After reporting their find to the guards, Walter, Winona, Whitney, and Winslow had quietly exited the Tower of London and crossed the Thames River over Tower Bridge. Presently they were walking upstream along the far bank.

"It's getting late," said Winona. "All in favor of staying in one of those excellent glass cabins in the London Eye say aye."

"Aye," the family said as one.

According to Whitney's guidebook, to reach the giant Ferris wheel they needed to keep following the southern embankment. Little did they know that the entire London Police Force not to mention the entire London TV and press corps was searching for them.

As the Wilsons walked at a carefree pace, they stopped at a newsstand. They were admiring the small compact structure when the stout man inside suddenly said, "Blyme! You're them! You're the blooming heroes. Blyme!"

The man held out the latest edition of the London Express newspaper.

"Fantabulous," said Winslow. "There's our picture."

"And the headlines say *Where are the Tower of London Heroes*?" said Whitney.

"Could that mean us?" said Winona.

"Blooming right it does," said the newsstand man. "The whole blooming police force is looking for you."

Walter grabbed the newspaper. As he read the article aloud, the man in the booth called the police. Things started happening fast after that. Within a minute three helicopters appeared in the sky over the Wilsons. Soon afterward, the sound of police sirens filled the air.

The first person to *find* the Wilsons, however, wasn't a bobby or a newsperson, but Samir, the cab driver. His black cab pulled up next to the newsstand.

"I found you, my friends," Samir called from the cab window. "Walter, Winona, Whitney, and Winslow

Wilson! I found you!"

"We didn't even know we were lost," said Walter.

"You are national heroes," said Samir. "You have spared the Royal Family much embarrassment and helped catch the jewel thieves."

"It sounds like a lot of fuss over nothing, Samir," said Winona.

"Too much beef by the Beefeaters," said Walter.

"You have no idea what a Royal humiliation it would have been for Queen Elizabeth to appear on TV wearing that fake jewelry," said Samir. "You have given me a wonderful plot idea for my new novel. My Writer's Block is unblocked. I can't wait to start writing."

At that moment, ten police cars, blue light flashing, pulled up behind Samir's taxi. At the same time, ten news vans stopped in front of the cab. Twenty police officers and twenty news people swarmed out of their vehicles.

For the next hour, the police questioned the Wilsons about the Tower heist, and the newspeople took their pictures and asked more questions. Finally, Walter raised his hands to say, "Sorry, good Londoners, but we must part. We must find a place to stay this Christmas Eve. We were on our way to the London Eye to see if space is still available."

By now, Scotland Yard knew about the Elevator Family and their accommodation preferences. They knew about the Otis room in the San Francisco Hotel, about Toll 4 over the Mississippi River, and about Harrods Department Store last night.

At this point, the Head of London Police, Captain Conrad Constable, stepped forward. He nodded and said, "Wilson Family, in appreciation for what you have done, Her Majesty the Queen, wishes to extend an

invitation to your family to stay with the royal family tonight at Buckingham Palace and join them tomorrow at their Christmas party."

"Fantabulous," said Winslow.

"The royal treatment," said Whitney.

"That's very kind of the queen," said Winona. "But her huge palace is not a place where we would be comfortable."

"Certainly not," said Walter. "Too big. Too many rooms. Perhaps, however, one of the small cabins in front of Buckingham Palace would be available. This morning we talked to a fine young man in a bushy tall hat who was staying in one."

After a moment of wondering, Captain Constable nodded. He pulled out his cell phone and said, "I'll see to it, right away, Mr. Wilson."

What followed was one of the grandest processions that the City of London has seen in many months. Word spread quickly throughout the city that the Wilson family, the family who had captured the Crown Jewel thieves, was about to be escorted from the

Thames River to Buckingham Palace. As a result, throngs of people soon lined the route to catch a glimpse of this extraordinary American family.

A fleet of police cars led the parade with their blues lights flashing. After this marched fifty Beefeaters who had hurried over from the Tower of London. Next rode forty of the Queen's Horse Guards on horseback wearing their fine red uniforms and shiny golden helmets. Finally came the heroes themselves riding in the back of Samir's black taxi. While Walter and Winona waved out one window, Winslow and Whitney waved out the other. The roar of the crowd was tremendous. Confetti and Christmas streamers filled the air.

"Merry Christmas! Merry Christmas!" the Wilsons called from the cab.

"Happy Christmas! Happy Christmas!" the Londoners returned.

A bigger and noisier crowd greeted the procession outside Buckingham Palace. When the taxi reached the front gates, two of the Queen's Foot Guards in their tall bushy hats pulled the gates open, and Samir drove up to a guardhouse in front of the palace.

The small hut had been fixed up splendidly. A small table with four chairs stood outside the front door. Four soft mattresses with soft silk sheets and a thick goose down quilt lay on the floor inside. A silver Christmas angel even stood on the peaked roof.

As the Wilsons stepped from the cab, trumpets blew. The family looked up to see Queen Elizabeth herself waving from a balcony.

"Only the best," said Walter, as he hung the Home Sweat Home sampler on the guardhouse wall. "Only the best will do for the Wilsons."

Early the next morning, Christmas morning, the Wilsons woke up to find the Queen's lady-in-waiting and head butler waiting for them outside the guardhouse. The table was set with the Queen finest breakfast china and silver.

Still in his pajamas, Walter stepped out of the little house and stretched his arms. "Excellent service at this palace," he said to the butler, who handed him a silk bathrobe.

"Happy Christmas, Mr. Wilson," the butler said. "Your breakfast is ready. Eggs and bangers."

Walter grumbled.

"*Bangers* is the British term for sausages, Dad," Whitney called from inside the hut.

Walter grumbled some more. "We'd rather have Cheerios and Corn Flakes, if you don't mind," he said.

"Very good, sir," said the butler. "Right away."

While the Wilsons ate, a man dress in a gray suit came out of Buckingham Palace and stood next to Walter.

"My name is Christopher, Her Majesty's private secretary," he said. "Her Majesty will deliver her Christmas message to the British people at 3 PM and Her Majesty wishes you to be in attendance. Her Majesty also wishes you to know that Her Majesty's Christmas party will begin shortly afterward. Please inform Her Majesty if there is anyone here in London that you wish to be included on Her Majesty's guest list."

Walter's eyes lit up. "Indeed there is," he said. "Tell Her Majesty that we have met many splendid people here in the UK."

During the morning, the Wilsons toured the palace, played with the Queen's five corgi dogs, and read more about the Crown Jewel plot in the newspapers.

"Says here that the jewelry crooks are spending Christmas in the Scotland Yard's slammer," said Walter.

"Says here that they made the fake Christmas Brooch themselves in the San Quentin prison metal shop," said Winona. "They cut the fake diamonds from empty Coke bottles."

"Says here that the entire United Kingdom would have been scandalized if the Queen wore the cheap glass brooch during her Christmas speech," said Whitney.

"Says here that the Prime Minister wishes to call us the Harrods Window Family from now on," said Winslow.

At 3:00, the Wilsons watched Queen Elizabeth II give her annual Christmas message to a TV camera. She wore a sparkly white dress, a diamond tiara, and, high up on her left shoulder, the Christmas Brooch with the Star of Bethlehem in the middle.

After the speech, the Wilsons were escorted into a grand ballroom where the Christmas party was in progress. The room was decorated tastefully with candles, garland, and large wreaths. A tall Christmas tree stood in one corner.

After being announced, the Wilsons joined the happy crowd, many who wore colorful paper crowns, a British Christmas custom. Music started, and the family recognized the sound. Kevin and Verity were singing *Holly and the Ivy* on a small stage. The Wilsons waved to them, and they nodded back.

Next, Mr. Brown and his wife, Bonnie, approached the Wilsons.

"Elevator Family, you've done it again," Mr. Brown said, pumping Walter's hand. "You're the talk of the entire European continent. By tomorrow Elevator Family merchandise will be selling like pancakes."

"Which, here in England, are not called pancakes at all, but *crepes*," said Walter with a grunt.

"Did you find Jack Christmas a job, Mr. Brown,"

asked Winona.

"That man is a natural salesman," said Bob Brown. "Look over there by the Christmas tree."

By the tree stood a long line of children including Becky Brown and various small dukes, duchesses, princes, and princesses. They were waiting to talk with Father Christmas who sat in a tall red chair.

"That's Jack!" said Whitney and Winslow said together

"The most authentic Father Christmas there ever was," said Mr. Brown.

Now an elegantly dressed man and woman approached the Wilsons.

"I'm Lord Harold Hashtag and this is my wife Lady Harold Hashtag," said the man. "Our new nanny, Mary, mentioned that she talked with you yesterday in Russell Square."

"Why yes," said Winona. "Mary seemed like an ideal nanny."

"Yes, we are very pleased with her," said Lady Hashtag. "Our daughter Victoria has never been happier. Whenever Mary laughs and smiles, little Victoria laughs and smiles. Whenever Mary claps her hands and wiggles her feet, Victoria claps and wiggles. All Christmas morning, they smiled, laughed, clapped, and wiggled together."

The party grew silent, as Queen Elizabeth and her husband, Prince Philip, entered the room. After shaking hands with a line of people, the Royals greeted the Wilsons. Walter and Winslow bowed, while Winona and Whitney curtsied as they had been instructed to do.

"We can't tell you how thankful we are to this family," said the Queen. "We wish to grant each of the Wilsons an Honorary British Knighthood."

Walter beamed. "That would make me Sir Walter," he said. "Sounds excellent."

"And I'll be Dame Winona," said Winona.

"And the twins will be Sir Winslow and Dame Whitney," said Prince Phillip.

"Perhaps after dinner we can all have a game of Pick-Up sticks," said the Queen. "We heard that Winslow is quite an expert at the game."

"He has the fingers of a jewel thief, ma'am," said Walter, and he instantly regretted the comment.

"Three cheers for Sir Walter, Dame Winona, Sir Winslow, and Dame Whitney Wilson," someone in the room shouted. "Hip, hip!"

"Hurrah!

"Hip, hip!"

"Hurrah!"

"Hip, hip!"

"Hurrah!"

"And a hippy hurrah to all of you," said Walter.

Shortly before dawn the next morning, Boxing Day, the Wilsons arose and packed up their bags. After all the fuss made over them the day before, they wanted to slip off this morning without any fanfare.

"We give you back your house," Walter said to the guard in the tall bushy hat who had paced back and forth before the guardhouse all night.

"Thanks for the lovely stay," said Winona.

"Please say goodbye to the Queen for us," said Winslow.

"And her five corgis," said Whitney.

Pulling their wheel luggage bags behind them, the Wilsons exited through Buckingham Palace's front gates. They planned to take the Underground to St. Pancras Train Station and catch the early morning Chunnel train to Paris, France.

At the Piccadilly Tube Station, this being a holiday, the Wilsons found the subway train nearly empty. They shared a car with one other passenger, a teenager who sat on an orange backpack.

"Alex!" the four Wilsons said together.

The American looked up and smiled.

"The Elevator Family!" he said. "You were all over the news on Christmas."

"And we're off to Paris right now on the morning Eurostar train," said Walter.

Alex beamed some more. "So am I," he said. "My world travels have begun."

"And you seem confident about it," said Winona.

"I feel bold and excited, thanks to the help you gave me," said Alex. "I'm ready for many big adventures."

"We're eager to reach the continent, too," said Winslow. "We saw pictures of some fantabulous kiosks in Paris that are right along the boulevards. They would be so cool to stay in."

"And in Switzerland, there are little moving cabins on wires that go right to the top of the Alps," said Whitney. "Wouldn't one of those be a great place to stay?"

The subway arrived at St. Pancras Station. The Wilsons and Alex rode the escalator up to the departure area.

"I hope to see as much of the world as I can in my year abroad," Alex said when they saw the morning light again.

"Drop us an e-mail while you're on the road," said Winona. "Perhaps our paths might cross again."

"Only the best," said Walter. "Yes, the world is full of big adventures, my boy."

"And small, cozy places to stay in," Winslow and Whitney said together.

Made in the USA
Coppell, TX
15 October 2023

22878761R00050